Peter Andre

THE UNOFFICIAL • BOOK •

Peter Andre

The Hunkiest Man Around

Virgin

First published in 1997 by Virgin Books,
an imprint of Virgin Publishing Ltd
332 Ladbroke Grove, London W10 5AH

A catalogue record for this book is available from the British Library

ISBN: 0 7535 0181 3

Printed and bound by Butler & Tanner

Designed by Slatter-Anderson
Text by Michael Heatley

Contents

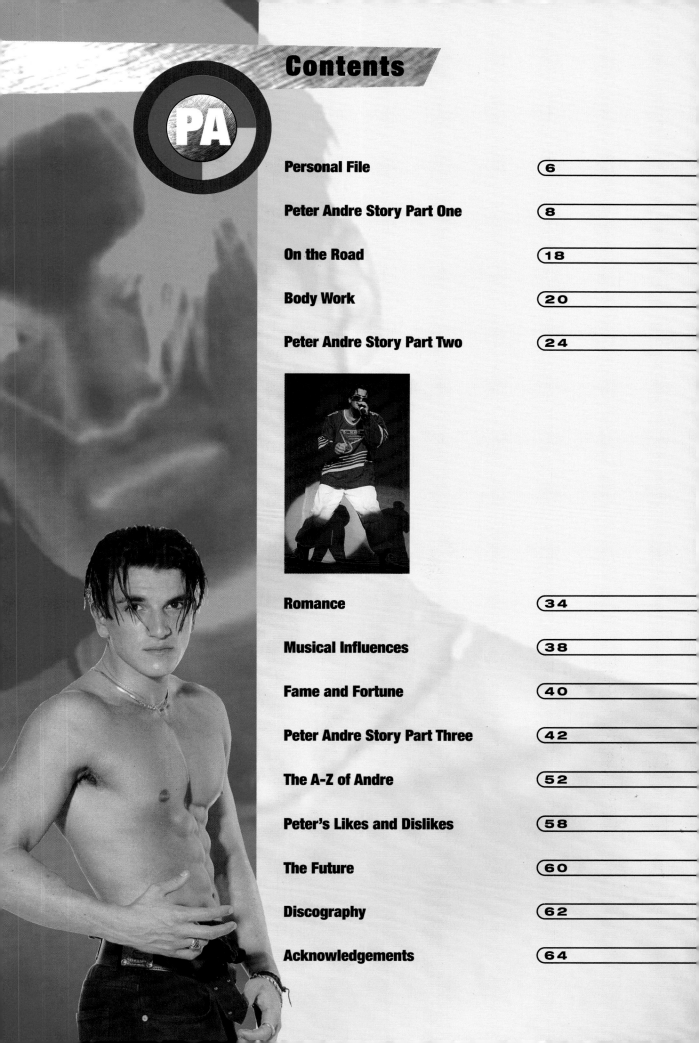

Personal File

Full Name:
Peter James Andrea

Date of Birth:
27 February 1973

Star Sign: Pisces

Family:
Has a total of four brothers and sisters: Michael (a DJ), Danny (a security guard), Chris (part of Peter's organisation) and Debbie, the youngest of the family.

Home:
Four-bedroom luxury flat in London's Docklands (behind high-security gates!)

Height:
Five feet 9 inches
(1.72 metres)

Weight:
9 stone 8 pounds (61 kg)

Colour of eyes: Brown

Colour of hair: Black

Hair Care:
Always buys his hair gel and stuff from an Afro shop because his hair's really curly and it's the best thing to straighten it.

Favourite Clothing:
Calvin Klein underwear

Favourite Drink:
Tia Maria and Coke – but even then only on a plane to get over fear of flying!

First Record Bought:
Michael Jackson's 'Off The Wall'

Favourite Music:
Jodeci, R Kelly, Mark Morrison

Favourite Films:
Twister, Independence Day

Previous Job:
Student, then briefly selling aftershave

Heroes: Jean-Claude Van Damme, Catwoman

School Yearbook Comments:
Most Likely To Succeed, Most Musically Inclined

Peter Andre Story Part One

WHEN THE HISTORY OF POP IS EVENTUALLY WRITTEN, THE MID 1990S WILL BE REMEMBERED AS THE ERA OF THE BOY BAND. FROM TAKE THAT TO BOYZONE, BACKSTREET BOYS TO 911, THE SCENE'S BEEN FLOODED WITH ALL-SINGING, ALL-DANCING, ALL-HARMONISING OUTFITS OUT TO CARVE THEIR OWN PLACE IN THE HEARTS OF THE RECORD-BUYING PUBLIC. EVEN THE SPICE GIRLS, THE FEMALE VERSION OF THE PHENOMENON, SOUGHT STRENGTH IN NUMBERS. IF YOU DIDN'T LIKE ONE, THERE WERE STILL FOUR MORE TO CHOOSE FROM...

It took someone special to break that mould. An individual talent so strong, so visually appealing that you'd need a heart of stone to resist him. And from the moment he first appeared on Top Of The Pops it was obvious

Peter Andre was that man. Peter had come to Britain from Australia in a quest for fame and fortune. But what many of his new-found fans may not have realised was that he was born in London on

27 February 1973 and lived in the suburb of Harrow from then until his family upped sticks and emigrated to the land down under, where he'd spent his teenage years. Mum and Dad first visited on holiday, and liked it so much they decided to stay. Another little-known bit of history is that his real name is Peter James Andrea: he changed the last bit to Andre when people kept pronouncing it An-dree-ah instead of On-dray-ah. His parents were born in Greece, which accounts for their son's exotic looks as well as his name.

The male Andre children grew up close – not least because they all shared the same bedroom! With four boys and only one girl (the youngest child, Debbie), the Andrea family was a very male-orientated one – but in Peter's eyes that was an advantage. He learned a lot from his brothers especially how they treated girlfriends.

As a kid at school in Australia it was schoolwork and not lessons in love that became top priority. But because he wasn't like the rest of them, he was ethnic-looking and spoke with a British accent, Peter soon found himself the centre of attention in the schoolyard at Benowa Primary School – and it wasn't for his performing skills. The kids used to gang up in big groups and try to bully him after school. The cold-shoulder treatment lasted about three years, during which time Peter found solace in singing. He just couldn't wait to get home and practice.

Peter admits to having been something of a shy lad, talkative enough when his friends were around him but painfully shy when it came to talking to strangers or the opposite sex. That's pretty amusing when you think of how he spends his time these days – but his love of performing to an audience would prove the key to his life.

When family and friends gathered for special occasions, Peter would take advantage of the situation to entertain them on home ground. His reception was universally warm...although his father would sometimes reprimand him for 'showing off' all the time.

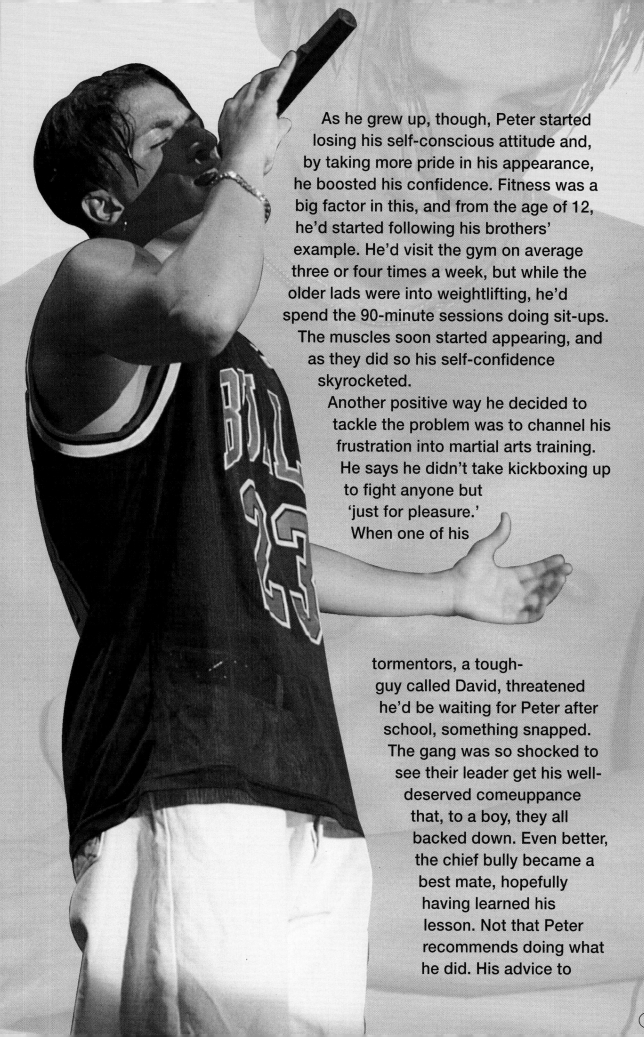

As he grew up, though, Peter started losing his self-conscious attitude and, by taking more pride in his appearance, he boosted his confidence. Fitness was a big factor in this, and from the age of 12, he'd started following his brothers' example. He'd visit the gym on average three or four times a week, but while the older lads were into weightlifting, he'd spend the 90-minute sessions doing sit-ups. The muscles soon started appearing, and as they did so his self-confidence skyrocketed.

Another positive way he decided to tackle the problem was to channel his frustration into martial arts training. He says he didn't take kickboxing up to fight anyone but 'just for pleasure.' When one of his tormentors, a tough-guy called David, threatened he'd be waiting for Peter after school, something snapped. The gang was so shocked to see their leader get his well-deserved comeuppance that, to a boy, they all backed down. Even better, the chief bully became a best mate, hopefully having learned his lesson. Not that Peter recommends doing what he did. His advice to

anyone being bullied is to tell somebody or phone Childline.

The opposite sex started catching Peter's eye around this time – and he thought he'd use his musical talents to get the girl of his dreams interested. Trouble was, she was 16 and he was just 13. One day on the school bus one of his mates suggested he serenaded her with the song 'Candy Girl' by New Edition. He only got as far as the first line before she went bright red. Wonder what she's thinking now…

Because he feared he'd be mocked, Peter disguised his ambition to be a professional musician and told people he wanted to be an architect. Schoolmates thought his musical tastes were old-fashioned. They were all into INXS, and he liked Marvin Gaye. He made a point of entering every talent contest he could find – and though he didn't succeed at first, he followed the old proverb and kept on trying! He used to analyse why he hadn't won. Was it his clothes? Was it his dancing? But instead of going home and giving up, Peter just kept practicing and getting better and better. He was true to his word – and a star-search he entered at the age of 17 proved the first rung of the showbiz ladder. He won top prize for his performance of Bobby Brown's 'Don't Be Cruel' and was awarded a recording contract with Mushroom Records, the label that would have success with Garbage and Dannii Minogue.

Bouyed by his big break, Peter was rushed into the studio and cut an album, simply entitled 'Peter Andre', which would soon go gold. He also notched up two spectacular singles successes: a revival of Brenton Wood's soul oldie 'Gimme Little Sign', which

not only reached Number 3 but became the best-selling Australian single of 1993, and ' Only One'. Peter had been so delighted to put out a record that, he claims, he was the very first person to go out and buy it!

With those hits came offers to tour – and for a man who reckons his success is down to his live performances, that urge would prove irresistible. His biggest thrill was supporting Madonna on her Australian tour. Bobby Brown, the king of swing whose song had brought him success in that all-important talent show, also took Peter on tour and from this time onwards they developed a healthy mutual respect for each other. And that was just as well, for their paths would cross in several times in the future.

One support opportunity Peter regretfully had to turn down was opening for the US rapper Vanilla Ice, who had a worldwide Number 1 in 1990 with 'Ice Ice Baby'. At the time he was going out with a singer called Tracy, and his inability to do the gig was to leave him with a severe case of a broken heart. She fell in love with one of Vanilla's dancers. He really swept her off her feet... Not for the first (or last) time, Peter picked himself up and started all over again, beginning a relationship with a girl called Kathy which would last for all of four years – so anyone thinking this boy's a flirt can think again! Meanwhile he carried on making a name for himself in a musical sense, touring Australia from coast to coast and picking up a huge fan following as he did so. Hordes of adoring fans greeted him at every live event. But somewhere in the back of his mind, he harboured thoughts of Britain - could he find sucess there too?

On the Road

Success has given Peter Andre a ticket to ride. Having lived on opposite sides of the globe, the past year has seen him 'joining the dots' on his personal atlas and visiting all points in between. 'I have been really busy lately, but it's good because if being busy means I'm going to be successful then I want to be busy! It was only when I sat down in First Class that I actually realised I've suddenly gone from being a nobody to being a somebody.'

That's the result of some special single-mindedness. Some people can sit around having a few beers and then go on stage…not Peter! He

likes to have the dressing room to himself for an hour before he goes on stage, an indication of his self-discipline. He does sit-ups and push-ups before the show to get the blood going. He claims it helps him think clearly and feel fit.

Peter's been a hit everywhere he goes – and while supporting Boyzone in Germany had 17,000 screaming girls out of their seats at the Munich Pop Festival. Now with the advent of his first solo tour he's got it made. He usually travels around in a Toyota Previa with blacked out windows, a mode of transport he much prefers to swanky limousines and the like. 'If people could see me,' he laughs, 'they'd probably throw tomatoes!'

Body Work

There are many pop stars whose face is their fortune – but few can rival Peter Andre, whose success as a singer has been matched by his status as pop's body beautiful. He doesn't drink, he doesn't smoke – his greatness weakness is being attracted to girls which as far as we can tell isn't an offence!

The first step to super-fitness came when he took up kickboxing in Australia. Now he has his own tailor-made fitness rountine to keep the King of Pecs in shape. He likes a tan, but restricts his use of sunbeds because he knows they're bad for you.

Diet's also important to his way of life, though he's finally got it into perspective and allows himself the occasional indulgence. For years he didn't eat junk food because he was a health fanatic but nowadays he does occasionally, of course, he works out extra hard the next day to compensate!

Many in the bodybuilding world have been tempted to take steroids. He's never taken drugs and doesn't intend to.

As for the future, Peter wants to put the spotlight on his musical talents – and if that means keeping his shirt on, then so be it. Even being super fit can't stop

accidents like the one that happened in Hong Kong when he fell downstairs and sprained his ankle. But though he had to cancel a roadshow performance he went out and met his fans anyway – proving that mental toughness is just as important as a muscular body!

"There's no point in

having great

muscles if you

don't have a

tan to show

yourself off."

P E T E R   A N D R E

Peter Andre Story Part Two

PETER TOOK HIS BIGGEST STEP TO STARDOM IN 1993 WHEN HE MADE THE DECISION TO MOVE BACK TO BRITAIN. HE ALSO DECIDED THAT IF HE WAS TO BE A HIT IN THE HOME COUNTRY HE'D LEFT WHEN HE WAS JUST TEN, HE'D DO IT WITH NEW MATERIAL – NOT JUST RE-RUN HIS OLD HITS FROM DOWN UNDER. IT WAS A BRAVE DECISION, AND ONE THAT WOULD PAY OFF HANDSOMELY – BUT IT MEANT HE HAD TO START AGAIN FROM SCRATCH.

How determined he was to succeed hit home when he popped into a newsagents soon after arriving in Britain and saw a bunch of schoolgirls crowded round the magazine racks lusting after soap star Dieter Brummer (another Aussie!). He had this real desire, that one day that was going to happen to him and from that minute onwards he started putting his thoughts into practice!

His base was a flat in Fulham, West London, very handy for the offices of his record label, Mushroom. His neighbours happened to be Ant and Dec, alias PJ and Duncan. Not that the boys from Byker Grove saw that much of Peter as he put 100% effort into his work. And the year ahead would indeed be a globetrotting one as he promoted his first UK-released album.

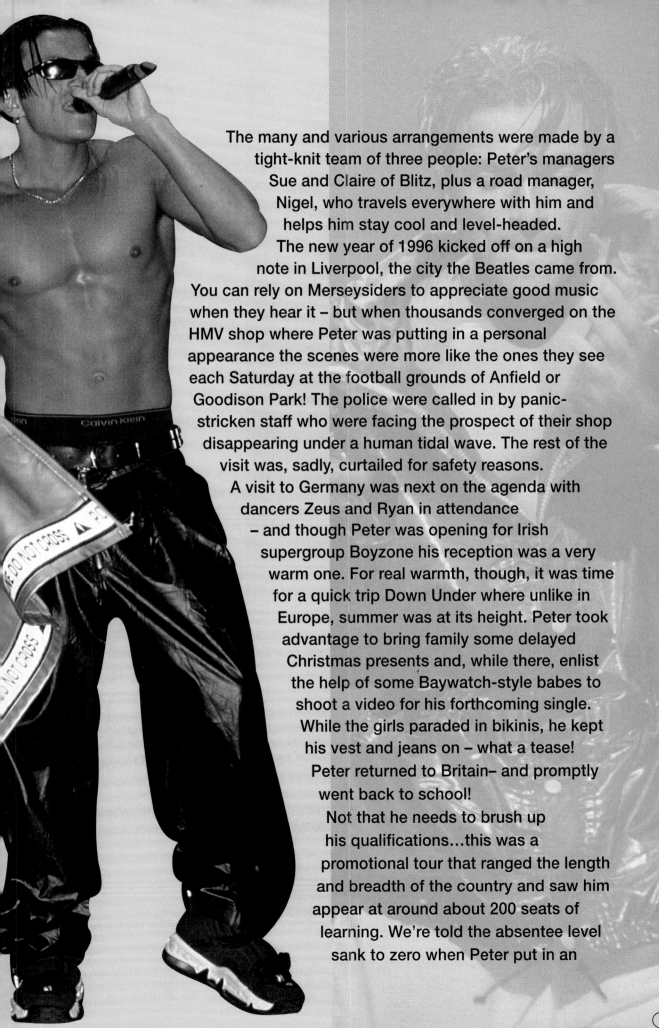

The many and various arrangements were made by a tight-knit team of three people: Peter's managers Sue and Claire of Blitz, plus a road manager, Nigel, who travels everywhere with him and helps him stay cool and level-headed.

The new year of 1996 kicked off on a high note in Liverpool, the city the Beatles came from. You can rely on Merseysiders to appreciate good music when they hear it – but when thousands converged on the HMV shop where Peter was putting in a personal appearance the scenes were more like the ones they see each Saturday at the football grounds of Anfield or Goodison Park! The police were called in by panic-stricken staff who were facing the prospect of their shop disappearing under a human tidal wave. The rest of the visit was, sadly, curtailed for safety reasons.

A visit to Germany was next on the agenda with dancers Zeus and Ryan in attendance – and though Peter was opening for Irish supergroup Boyzone his reception was a very warm one. For real warmth, though, it was time for a quick trip Down Under where unlike in Europe, summer was at its height. Peter took advantage to bring family some delayed Christmas presents and, while there, enlist the help of some Baywatch-style babes to shoot a video for his forthcoming single. While the girls paraded in bikinis, he kept his vest and jeans on – what a tease!

Peter returned to Britain– and promptly went back to school!

Not that he needs to brush up his qualifications...this was a promotional tour that ranged the length and breadth of the country and saw him appear at around about 200 seats of learning. We're told the absentee level sank to zero when Peter put in an appearance…

Behind the scenes, the finishing touches were being put to Peter's long-awaited album – not in London, New York or even Sydney as you might think but Denmark, where producers Cutfather and Joe were very much on the case. If you're not familiar with the names, look on the back of your copy of Mark Morrison's chart-topping 'Return Of The Mack'.

So, after recording the final few tracks, it was time to release a single – 'Only One', which hit the racks on 4 March. It soon shot into the Top 20, abetted by Peter's first ever appearance on Top Of The Pops (video recorders countrywide whirred into action!). Meanwhile Down Under he'd got the New Zealand charts in a stranglehold by monopolising both the top two positions with 'Mysterious Girl' and his version of Kool and the Gang's disco classic 'Get Down On It'. Peter paid a visit to celebrate… and was promptly greeted by 6,000 screaming fans who brought the city to a standstill!

Popping over to Australia en route to England, Peter fitted in an appearance at the opening of Brisbane's Hard Rock Café. Once in England again though, it was back on the road with a series of roadshows organised by Mizz magazine – which, his fans all agreed, were not to be Mizz-ed! Something else many people caught was Pete playing TV host on Channel 4. While half of Britain was dreaming of waking up to Peter's smiling face, there he was on the Big Breakfast leaping about like he'd been up all night (which he more or less had!).

However wonderful the year had been to date, it was all just a curtain-raiser to the events of May when 'Mysterious Girl' finally got its UK release. You couldn't have blamed cable TV viewers for having worn out their rewind button, because the video to the song had hit the top of their charts as long ago as January – and, what was more, stayed there a whole nine weeks! With such a groundswell of demand, it was no surprise that the single bulleted into the chart at Number 3 behind fellow Aussie-turned-Brit Gina G's Eurovision entry

and would prove so popular Peter would use a similar sun and sea theme for the follow-up, this time shot in the States. And maybe it was no coincidence that the strangest of many performances of the single that Peter was called upon to give, also featured a lot of water.

Unlike the tropical climes he was used to, though, he was asked to sing in the middle of a lake at Windsor's Legoland theme park. Contrary to what you may have heard, he doesn't walk on water – a barge provided the most unusual floating stage he's ever graced! The cause was a good one too…GMTV's Get Up and Give campaign.

Having lent his name to a favourite charity, Peter had earned a rest – and got one in June, jetting off to Cyprus to top up his all-over tan. While there, he met model Nikki Heard, who would be the love interest in his life for the next few months. They

and the Lightning Seeds' football anthem on 1 June. The following fortnight saw it go one place better – and, though it couldn't quite dislodge 'Killing Me Softly', it kept Peter's name in the charts for the whole summer period. Peter Andre had arrived…

The video to 'Mysterious Girl' clearly had a lot to do with its success. It had been shot in exotic Thailand,

were first seen in public at the première of the blockbusting film Independence Day. If Peter was acting the perfect gentleman by keeping things under wraps, it was all the more disappointing that, when it ended, details of their affair were splashed all over the Sunday papers.

Next stop was Los Angeles, the music capital of the world, where his task was a video shoot for the upcoming single – the one, as it turned out, that would take him to the very top. On his return to Britain he was scheduled to tour the country, again as special guest of Boyzone, but instead found himself in hospital on the wrong end of a food poisoning scare!

Basically he'd become dehydrated because he'd been working such long hours and then on top of that he got food poisoning. There was one point where the doctors said if he went on stage he could have a heart attack because his blood pressure was so high. Thankfully, our super-fit hero shook off the bug and was back out there pumpin' and prancin' with the Boyz. The tour rocked on through July, with Peter getting just as many screams as the headliners. And when he stepped out solo in the open air at Capital Radio's Roadshow in London, it just took one shrug of the shoulders to expose that famous body – and see him all but submerged under a human wave as a fanatical crowd surged past security and towards the stage. It really was turning out to be a summer to remember!

Meanwhile 'Mysterious Girl' – boosted by its video and that infectious Bubbler Ranx reggae-style rap – just wouldn't leave the best-seller listings.

When it passed 275,000 sales it replaced Garbage's 'Stupid Girl' as the Mushroom label's British best-seller. Better than that, by spending 11 weeks in the Top 5, it eventually clocked up a total of 750,000 UK copies sold. It seemed that the only way for Peter to get another single out would be to delete it – which is exactly what happened! Despite that less than glamorous end, 'Mysterious Girl' would, for millions of music fans worldwide, be the summer sound of 1996.

August saw Peter clocking up the air miles once again,

jetting out to Korea and Thailand before hitting the holiday island of Ibiza for GMTV's Fun In The Sun spot. And holed up in a five-star hideaway that had previously played host to fellow superstars George Michael, Madonna and Michael Jackson, he was clearly impressed. He pledged to return to the place ...with his swimming trunks, presumably...he'd been in such a hurry he forgot to pack them and spent all weekend in his Calvin Klein boxer shorts!

But though GMTV had made him more than welcome, the television highlight of the year was yet to come. On returning home, he found a very welcome invitation on the doormat, complete with a BBC postmark. Would Peter like to introduce Top Of The Pops ? Would he ever...

That very special appearance took place in early September – and with the re-formed New Edition back in the charts with 'Hit Me Off', it gave Pete the chance to introduce one of his biggest musical idols, Bobby Brown, the star he'd opened the show for in Australia all those years back.

But even Bob had to stand back and watch in wonder as 'Flava', released on 8 September, shot straight in at the very top of the chart a week later thanks to initial sales of nearly 130,000.

The 'Flava' video, shot in Los Angeles, featured Pete dancing with a whole posse of bronzed babes, romping in the surf and working out at a beach-side gym between takes. With his blue oversize shirt seemingly unable to stay on those muscular shoulders, it certainly seemed to give the track a special boost. And when 'Flava' hit the top to end the Spice Girls' all-conquering seven-week reign, it succeeded where George Michael, Robbie Williams and the Fugees had failed.

He'd done it at last...and performing at the Top Of The Pops weekend at Wembley Arena on 13-14 September was the icing on the cake. His appearance, singing his two biggest hits to a huge nationwide TV audience, helped raise £150,000 for Childline.

Peter had arrived and Britain welcomed him back with open arms.

When it comes to pin-ups, Peter Andre is every girl's dream. But what is it that turns him on? His ideal woman is Halle Berry of Flintstones fame. He describes her as '100 per cent babe'. He says, 'I always think there's got to be the right woman out there somewhere, just waiting for me to find her. And when I do, she should really be prepared for some love.'

Denise Van Outen, presenter of TV's Massive and Big Breakfast, certainly thinks Peter's got a lot to offer. She went on a 'date' with him for BIG magazine in summer 1996, and returned to say that she thought Peter was the perfect date.

The press are keen to play matchmaker – too keen, in some cases! When Peter was last in Australia, it was reported on the radio that Julia Roberts was flying into the country to meet up with a secret lover. And who was cited as the secret lover? Only our very own Peter.

If you want to be a hit with Peter, just turn on the smouldering gaze – it gets him every time! 'If a girl gives me that certain look, a look of utter seduction, it knocks me off my feet. I really get turned on when she's dead confident about herself and says just what's on her mind. I like straight-forward girls who are really down-to-earth.'

Peter's looking for someone who's confident and happy with themselves, and is a good conversationalist. Physical attraction is a bonus but Peter's view is that friendship is far more important. And he is a loyal guy too. He says he would never two-time a girl if it was a serious relationship. Peter's dream date would be going out to an intimate candlelit dinner, where he could really reveal his inner self. Should you be that lucky girl, Peter's got plans for you. He wants to be married by the time he's 28, so he's got five years to search for the ideal woman. As for little Andres, he wants one boy and one girl. Coming from a large family, his grandad had 17 kids, his dad is one of 12, and Peter is one of six, you might think he'd want lots of kids, but he say he'd be happy with just two. Anyone for happy families?

Musical Influences

As a child, Peter woke up to music – quite literally! His Dad would set the radio alarm for 7.30am every morning and it would be the sounds of Stevie Wonder or Luther Vandross that would wake him. His earliest idol was Michael Jackson – and by listening to his music he became interested in the music of the 1960s and the classic years of Tamla Motown.

Marvin Gaye, the Four Tops and the Supremes all started to find a place in his heart and record collection – and that marked him out as different in rock-crazed Australia. At school, all the kids were into INXS while Peter's idols were all black singers.

He stuck with his preferences, and was rewarded when he went on to win a talent contest with a song by New Edition's Bobby Brown. Current favourites include swingbeat artists like TLC and Mark Morrison (with whom he shares a producer), and that should soon come out even more in his future recorded work. Peter says his next album will be even more R&B.

Fame and Fortune

Don't tell Peter Andre it's tough being a star – for him it's the best job ever. He can still remember a time back in Australia when he was sitting down telling his family he'd do anything to be out there working and singing his songs. The only drawback to success is the long hours and lack of sleep. But as they say - no pain, no gain.

When off duty, Peter will go out of his way to avoid publicity – he recently turned down the opportunity to open a supermarket because he thought he'd 'feel a bit strange'. And while he accepts there's a price to be paid for being a public figure, he's clear on where he draws the line. His home is his private domain, photographers aren't welcome there but when he is out and about it is all part of the course of being famous.

You have to put up with a good deal of adverse comment when you're a pop star - people can mistake a winning smile for a sign of insincerity. In the early days in Australia and New Zealand people thought Peter's smile was just an act. He prefers to confront his critics face to face when guys in the street tell him his songs are not good, he replies with that famous grin and tells them he's writing his songs for their girlfriends and not them!

Peter Andre Story Part Three

IT HAD TAKEN MOST OF THE YEAR TO BE RECORDED, MIXED AND PACKAGED – NOW IT WAS TIME FOR HIS FIRST UK ALBUM TO BE UNLEASHED ON AN UNSUSPECTING WORLD.

Needless to say by now, 'Natural' copied 'Flava' by going in at pole position, having been launched with a very swanky party at London's Natural History Museum. It was the Mushroom label's first UK Number 1, (Garbage's self-titled debut having peaked at Number 6 earlier in the year) and by its second chart week had broken the six-figure sales barrier to gain its performer a well-deserved gold disc.

Peter had taken a hand in the writing of 11 of the album's 13 tracks – a sharp reminder to the critics that this man was no-one's puppet. The exceptions were

'Message To My Girl', written by Crowded House guitarist Neil Finn and 'Get Down On It', the big hit from down under that was included as a 'PS'. Despite its great club vibe, Peter wasn't keen on issuing a cover version of the Kool classic as a single, feeling he didn't want people to be confused about the direction of his music. That song also marked his debut as a producer, hinting at future developments.

Two of the songs, 'Tell Me When' and 'You Are', were written by Peter on his own, while the others included various co-writers including soul singer Glen

Goldsmith and, for 'All I Ever Wanted', the team of Deni Lew, Nicky Graham and Wayne Hector, the same team that had helped PJ and Duncan transform themselves from children's TV stars to adult chart favourites. This added a variety that kept things fresh from song to song.

A bewildering number of studios – well over ten, including ones in Copenhagen and Melbourne – were used to record 'Natural', together with an equally confusing number of musicians. But the good news was that the whole project had a real air of unity about it that came from the man who fronted the show.

Collectors were quick to snap up a limited edition CD that came in a silver tin engraved with the initials PJA, but there was no doubt that whatever version made it into your collection this was one of the must-

buys of the year. Peter and Boyzone had now gone their separate ways after their successful tours of earlier in the year. Peter was now far too big in commercial terms to open the show for anybody...but the MTV awards on 14 November saw the two parties concerned say goodbye in the most spectacular and soulful way possible. They teamed up to set Alexandra Palace alight with a magnificent medley of Motown

favourites, lead vocals switching between Peter, Ronan and Stephen with practiced ease. Everyone was clearly having a ball, and their performance was the undisputed

highlight of a star-studded spectacle. Peter's fans had enjoyed a blinding year all right, but there were more fireworks to come in late November with the release of 'I Feel You' on the 25th. To no-one's surprise, by now, it knocked the Prodigy and their pet alligator straight off the Number 1 position – and Peter celebrated his second chart-topper in three months

in style on the Smash Hits Roadshow tour which was busily criss-crossing the country at the time.

The video for 'I Feel You' was quite a departure from what fans had come to expect. Instead of the usual winning combination of an exotic location, sun, sea and sexy ladies, the scene was very different – an old nursery school in the south London suburb of Camberwell! But staying indoors didn't mean any lack of action, as events were soon to prove... To suit the single's late November-early December release date, fake snow had been scattered on the windowpanes to give a wintry vibe, while Peter stared sultrily out through the glass thinking of his departed lover. In flashbacks, Peter and Charlene (the lucky lady playing his screen girlfriend) would be seen having a 'bit of a romp' as Peter characteristically put it. So much of a romp, in fact, that a separate, saucier video was also cut which, he suggested, would only be shown 'after the watershed'.

The result, whichever way you looked at it, was the Christmas single of the year – with the best ever video! Despite competition from the Spice Girls, the Dunblane charity record and Sir Cliff Richard, Peter had been first to top the December charts – and was in no mood to be deposed!

Christmas, of course, means presents, and Peter was looking lucky when he picked up three nominations at the Smash Hits Poll Awards. The titles of Best Male Singer, Best Newcomer and Most Fanciable Person were up for grabs –

and Peter took the first by a mile from ex-Take Thatter Gary Barlow. In a touch of friendly rivalry, he separated Boyzone buddies Ronan and Steve in the Most Fanciable listings – and while the Spice Girls took Best New Act honours, Peter beat them to the 'gong' in the Best Album Cover stakes, ending the Awards with two golden globes. There was no doubt about it – 1996 had been nothing short of a memorable year. Peter went from being a well-kept secret known only to the viewers of The Box cable channel in January, to a pop sensation inspiring over 400,000 fan letters by year's end. In fact, the local postmen heaved a sigh of relief (instead of sacks of mail) when warm-hearted Peter pleaded with his fans to donate the cost of a Christmas card to the homeless charity Shelter instead of sending one to him! With a truly golden twelve months to his credit and the new year of 1997 stretching out before him, Peter

Andre spent an enjoyable Christmas contemplating successes to come. One thing he wouldn't be doing so much of any more – on television at least – would be whipping his top off. He would, however, continue to do it on stage – and that was good news for the thousands who'd already invested in tickets for the Natural Tour, dates for which had already been inked in on his 1997 engagements diary.

His first headlining jaunt across the UK was scheduled to kick off in Preston on 26 February and end in Southport on 29 March. Highlight of the month-long tour was the 24 March appearance at London's Royal Albert Hall, time-honoured venue for the Last Night of the Proms. We couldn't guarantee Peter's fans would be waving Union Jacks and singing 'Land Of Hope And Glory', but it was certain the grand old building would be rocked to its very foundations! While Peter was already thinking ahead to his next album, signs were that 'Natural' would continue to be the 'Flava' on the musical menu, so to speak, for some time to come. So though that meant fans might have to wait a while for new material, at least the pop world would have the chance to catch their hero in person.

With the Natural Tour scheduled to move on to Europe, Australia and the Far East after its British leg, chances were that the next 12 months would see the name of Peter Andre known throughout the world.

If Peter had rocked the globe in 1996, he'd moved something else too – himself! The legendary flat on the floor above Ant and Dec became a magnet for fans who'd discovered where their idol lived. It's nice to be sought after but hard working stars need their sleep (as did all the other tenants in the block. To spare the feelings of all concerned Peter took himself off to an even posher gaff. This was in London's exclusive Docklands redevelopment area, where fans were kept politely at arm's length by some high-tech security gates.

The new flat has four-bedrooms, but anyone thinking Peter might be lonely in such a large apartment should think again! He's got two of his brothers to move in with him, while the other room is scheduled to be transformed into a gym. Peter's physique has become so legendary that even the stars want to know just how he keeps in shape. At the 'Independence Day' Party Mick Hucknall approached Peter for some inside information on his sit-up technique. The two singers hit it off with Peter having to draw little diagrams on a scrap of paper.

Having recruited people in his organisation he could trust to keep his feet fixed firmly on the ground, Peter isn't about to have his head turned by what he's achieved so far. The first flush of success can be fantastic but it's still too early to get carried away with partying. Peter knows at this stage that its best to keep his head down and keep working hard. It's hard to get there, but it's even harder to stay there.

With that attitude, the boy from Britain …Australia…er, Britain…should go far!

The A-Z of Andre

A is for **Andre:** The gorgeous hunk himself and for **Accent:** A distinctive one which is a mixture of Aussie and English. There's also **Ashley Cadell** who co-wrote 'To The Top' with Peter and played all the instruments on it.

B is for **Blitz** management, the team who help keep Peter on schedule; **Brothers**, of which he has four, the **Body** which has helped make his fortune and the **Box** cable TV channel which did so much to help break Peter's career in early '96.

C is for **Candles**, which Peter puts in the recording studio when lights are dimmed to create an atmosphere; **Chest**, his self-confessed sexiest part of his body, **Calvin Klein**, his favoured underwear and **Curly**...the natural state of his hair unless gelled into submission!

Dark glasses

D is for **Docklands**, where Peter currently resides with two of his brothers; **Diet:** Important for keeping his vital statistics in check and **Dark glasses**, an ever-present part of his off-stage disguise.

E is for **Elvis**, whose hair Peter envies – jet black and smooth and **Exercise**, something that's part of his everyday routine.

F is for **Fulham**, the area of London where Peter first settled after returning to Britain, **'Flava'** the first Number 1 single...and **Food poisoning** which he caught in the States after shooting the 'Flava' video.

G is for **Glen Goldsmith**, a talented singer who co-writes many songs with Peter, **Greece** where Pete's parents come from and **GMTV** whose Fun in the Sun gave him a chance to shine.

H is for **Harrow**, the area where Peter lived his early years, **Hong Kong** where he nearly broke his ankle and **Heartbreak**, something Peter knows only too well.

I is for **Inspirational, Individual** and **Interesting** – all adjectives you'd associate with Peter Andre. Then there's **Ibiza**, Peter's all-time favourite holiday spot.

J is for filmstar **Julia Roberts**, one of many screen babes linked with Peter – not all truthfully! – **Jodeci**, his favourite R&B act, and **Junk food**, a little indulgence once in a while after which he exercises twice as hard!

K is for **Kiss** – Peter's first was with a girl called Miranda when he was six. Also **Kids** – Peter wants two when he settles down – and **Kickboxing**, one of the martial arts in which he excels.

L is for **London**, Peter's new home, and **Los Angeles**, where he filmed the 'Flava' video by the side of the surf.

M is for **Motorbike**, which he keeps in Australia. Also **Mirrors**, which adorn his bedroom and **MTV** the satellite music channel which fell in love with Pete's pecs.

N is for **Nallie**, an all-purpose Australian surfing term meaning 'wicked or excellent' which Peter uses a lot. And **'Natural'**, the title of his Number 1 album.

O is for **'Oh Girl'**, the original title of the track **'Only One'**, and the **O Zone**, whose Jamie and Jayne have given Peter such great support in past months.

P is for **Peter** (who else?!), **Preston**, where he kicked off his first solo tour in February 1997. **Passion** which he inspires in his fans and **Pectorals**, the muscles he's internationally famed for.

Q is for Michael Jackson's producer **Quincy Jones**, a musical hero who may just produce Peter's next album and **Quality**, the feeling that runs through every track Peter creates.

R is for **Recording**, a process that took up much of Peter's time and energy in 1996... **Raunchy** an adjective often used to describe his lyrics, **Roses** the flowers he sends to his girlfriends, and **Romance**, the subject that's close to his heart.

A is for Andre: The gorgeous hunk himself

S is for **Sly**, one of the two dancers he works with live, **Sixpack**, the name his body answers to and **Swingbeat**, the muscular one's top choice of listening.

T is for **Top Of The Pops** which Peter's graced as both performer and presenter, **Toast** which Bubbler Ranx contributed to 'Mysterious Girl' and **Tin**, the metal box a limited edition of 'Natural' was packaged in.

U is an initial that Peter uses frequently in lyrics and song titles – a bit like Prince! – as in **Show U Somethin'**.

V is for **Van Outen**, Denise of that ilk, who dated Peter for a magazine story and rated him a real gentlemen. And **Videos**, the sun, sea and surf-packed clips that sent his chart status soaring.

W is for **Women**, the inspiration for many of Peter's songs... **Washboard** (that stomach, what else?) and **Walkman**, his constant companion while travelling to eat up the hours.

X is for the **Xtra** bonus tracks Peter puts on all his singles and the **X-rated** version of the 'I Feel You' video, which Peter claims is for late night – you'll know what he means soon enough.' X-actly!

Y is for **Youth** which Peter at 23 still has on his side.

Z is for **Zeus** one of his backing dancers on stage

pectorals, body

sixpack, washboard, chest

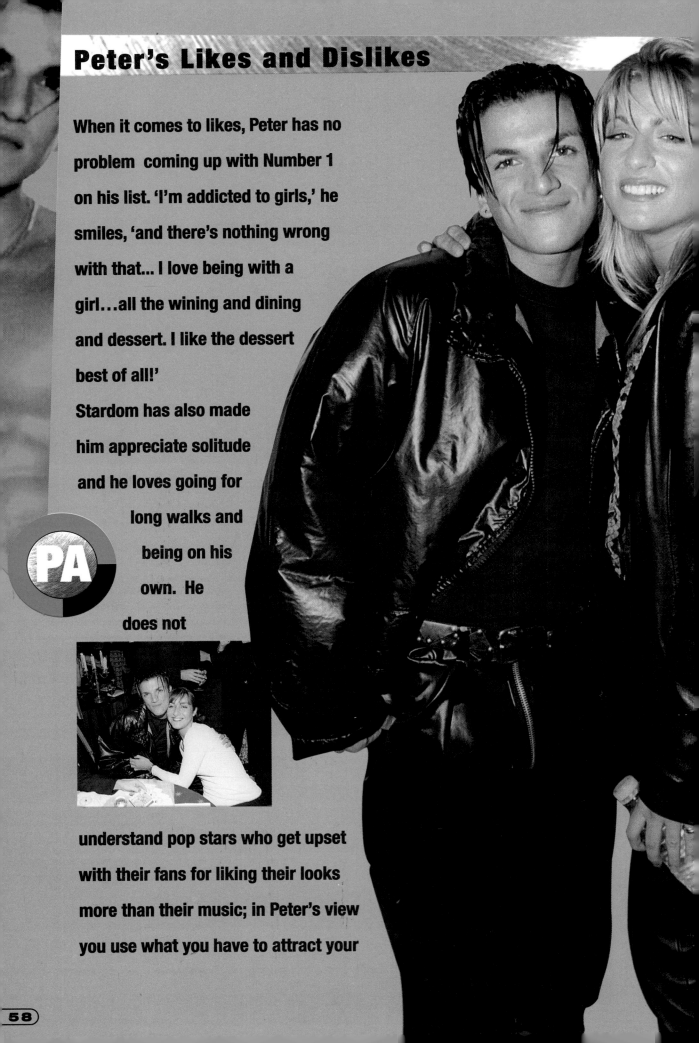

Peter's Likes and Dislikes

When it comes to likes, Peter has no problem coming up with Number 1 on his list. 'I'm addicted to girls,' he smiles, 'and there's nothing wrong with that... I love being with a girl…all the wining and dining and dessert. I like the dessert best of all!'

Stardom has also made him appreciate solitude and he loves going for long walks and being on his own. He does not understand pop stars who get upset with their fans for liking their looks more than their music; in Peter's view you use what you have to attract your

PA

fans and through time your talent will eventually show through. If you haven't got talent you shouldn't be making music anyway.

Another pet hate is spiders – especially a breed of the creatures called Hunsmen which thrive in Australia. If you annoy them they jump as high as eight metres and they can bite you! His own method of dealing with spiders is to use hairspray on them, though it makes him feel guilty. Quite right too – what a waste!

Something else he can live without is spooky rollercoaster rides at fairgrounds – because this is a man who likes to know exactly where he's going. Dreams, too, are enough to put the wind up our Peter. One recent one had him falling off a cliff backwards just before he hit the bottom he woke up and fell out of bed!

On the other hand, some far nicer dreams are to be had in-between the black satin sheets he likes next to him in bed. The very best are to do with his career, such as the 'ultimate dream' of playing Wembley Stadium. He really likes to dream of more success. And why not?

The Future

For a man who spends the hour before he goes on stage concentrating on the job in hand, Peter Andre is single-minded about what he wants from life – both personally and musically. Let's take the last first.

To produce the next album Babyface and Jermaine Dupri, who both worked with TLC have been approached. The name of legendary producer Quincy Jones has also been mentioned. A truly great honour for a new star. Astrologically speaking, Peter's a Pisces, which means he's amazingly romantic, somewhat disorganised, prone to being emotional – and, though curious about the future, might not find making choices easy. So should he be given the chance to broaden his career horizons, for instance with a major film role, expect him to say yes…but be unable to give up any of his other exploits. Maybe he really needs a 48-hour day!

The future should see Peter making friends with the catwalk, not to mention

hobnobbing with a supermodel or two. Clothes designer Calvin Klein has approached Peter to model for him, which he thinks may happen in 1998. Although he's never thought of himself as a model it's a demanding job that puts him on another level and as with everything else he does he is prepared to give it his best shot.

SINGLES

'Only One'

CD 1: D 1307 b/w Only One Rapino Brothers Club Mix/Gonna Get To You/Peter Andre Exclusive Interview Part 1

CD 2: DX 1307 b/w Only One Rapino Brothers Dub Mix/Let's Get It On/ Peter Andre Exclusive Interview Part 2

MC Single: C 1307.

Released March 1996. Highest chart position: 16.

'Mysterious Girl' featuring Bubbler Ranx

CD 1: D 2000/b/w Mysterious Girl Radio Edit/Mysterious Girl R&B Shank Mastermix/Mysterious Girl Malibu Mix/Mysterious Girl Turn It Up Extended Mix CD 2: DX 2000/b/w Mysterious Girl Radio Edit/Mysterious Girl Jupiter's Swing Mix/Mysterious Girl Descent and Submerged Remix/Mysterious Girl Bag of Tricks Mix

MC Single: C 2000.

Released May 1996. Highest chart position: 2.

'Flava'

CD 1: D 2003/b/w Flava Radio 7 Inch Edit//Flava Benz Mix/Flava Richie P Mix/Flava Crichton & Morris 12-Inch Mix/ncludes Free Songwords Poster

CD 2: DX 2003 b/wFlava Radio 7 Inch Edit/Flava Slammin' 12 Inch Edit/Flava Richie P Mix/Flava Crichton & Morris/ Flava Jungle Mix 12-Inch Mix/Includes Free Songwords Poster

MC Single: C 2003.

Released September 1996. Highest chart position: 1.

'I Feel You'

CD 1: D 1521b/w I Feel Your Radio Edit/I Feel You The Ruby Centre Mix/You Are Part One/I Feel You Cruisin' Mix/Includes Free Songwords Poster

CD 2: DX 1521b/w I Feel You Radio Edit/I Feel You Mark 'Crypt' Lewis Mix Oh Girl ('Only One' Original Pop Mix '93)/Includes Free Tour Poster

MC Single: C 1521.

Released November 1996. Highest chart position: 1.

ALBUMS

'Natural'

CD: D 2005/CD 2: DX 2005/LP: L 2005/MC: C 2005.

Released September 1996. Highest chart position: 1

Flava – Natural – Mysterious Girl – I Feel You – You Are (Part Two) – All I Ever Wanted – Show U Somethin' – To The Top – Tell Me When – Only One – Message To My Girl – Turn It Up – Get Down On It

Acknowledgements

Picture Credits

All Action
Nick Tansley: 5 (left), 6, 7, 14 (background), 20 (bottom), 22, 39 (bottom), 40, 53, 57
Dave Hogan: 9, 12, 13 (bottom), 44, 45, 47, 54, 58 (left, main), 59 (top)
John Gladwin: 10, 13 (top), 18, 19, 27, 28, 29 (top and bottom), 30, 31, 34 (bottom), 35, 43, 46 (bottom), 48, 52, 59 (bottom)
Eamonn Clarke:11
Simon Meaker: 14 (inset), 15, 49, 63
Splash: 20 (top), 56
Doug Peters: 5, 26, 34 (top), 38, 39 (top), 42, 46 (top), 50, 51, 55 (top, middle) 64
O'Brien/Peters: 41
All Action 16,17

LFI
Paul Cox: 1,2, 32, 33, 36, 60, 61
David Fisher: 25,55 (bottom)

The Publisher would like to thank the following publications for their permission to use quotes in the book: p.18 (top) TV Hits; (bottom) Big!; p.23 Big!; p.34 (top) Big!; (bottom) Live and Kicking Magazine, BBC Worldwide Limited 1996; p.58 TV Hits.